MAGIC EYE® BOOK

3D Magical Creatures, Beasts and Beings

Harry Potter Magic Eye Book: 3D Magical Creatures, Beasts and Beings copyright © 2010 by Warner Bros. Entertainment Inc. Magic Eye images copyright © 2010 by Magic Eye Inc. All rights reserved. Printed in China. No part of this book may be used or reproduced in any manner whatsoever without written permission except in the case of reprints in the context of reviews. For information, write Andrews McMeel Publishing, LLC, an Andrews McMeel Universal company, 1130 Walnut Street, Kansas City, Missouri 64106.

10 11 12 13 14 WKT 10 9 8 7 6 5 4 3 2 1

ISBN: 978-0-7407-9770-5

Magic Eye 3D Artists: Cheri Smith, Sam Jones, and Dawn Zimiles

www.andrewsmcmeel.com

Harry Potter™

MAGIC EYE® BOOK

3D Magical Creatures, Beasts and Beings

Andrews McMeel Publishing, LLC

Kansas City • Sydney • London

INSTRUCTIONS #2
FOR DIVERGING YOUR EYES
(focusing beyond the image)
To reveal the hidden 3D illusion, hold the center of the image *right up to your nose*. It should be blurry. Focus as though you are looking *through* the image into the distance. *Very slowly* move the image away from your face until you begin to perceive depth. Now hold the page still and the hidden image will slowly appear.

MAGIC EYE "FLOATERS"
Magic Eye "Floaters" are another type of Magic Eye 3D illusion. "Floaters" can first be viewed in 2D, and then, by using the standard Magic Eye viewing techniques, "Floaters" will appear to float in 3D space. Floaters and Magic Eye hidden illusions may be combined. (See page 14.)

ADDITIONAL VIEWING INFORMATION
Discipline is needed when a Magic Eye 3D illusion starts to "come in" because at that moment you will instinctively try to look at the page rather than looking through it, or before it. If you "lose it," start again.

There are two methods for viewing Magic Eye images: diverging your eyes (focusing beyond the image) and converging your eyes (focusing before the image or crossing your eyes). All the Magic Eye images in this book have been created to be viewed by diverging your eyes.

INSTRUCTIONS #1
FOR DIVERGING YOUR EYES
(focusing beyond the image)
To reveal the hidden 3D illusion, hold the center of the image *right up to your nose*. It should be blurry. Focus as though you are looking *through*

the image into the distance. *Very slowly* move the image away from your face until the two squares above the image turn into three squares. If you see four squares, move the image farther away from your face until you see three squares. If you see one or two squares, start over!

When you *clearly see three squares*, hold the page still, and the hidden image will slowly appear. Once you perceive the hidden image and depth, you can look around the entire 3D image. The longer you look, the clearer it becomes. The farther away you hold the page, the deeper it becomes.

If you converge your eyes (focus before the image or cross your eyes) and view an image created for diverging your eyes, the depth information comes out backward, and vice versa! This means if we intend to show a dragon flying in front of a cloud, if you converge your eyes you will see a dragon-shaped hole cut into the cloud! Another common occurrence is to diverge or converge your eyes twice as far as is needed to see the hidden image; for example, when you see four squares above the image instead of three, you will see a scrambled version of the intended hidden image.

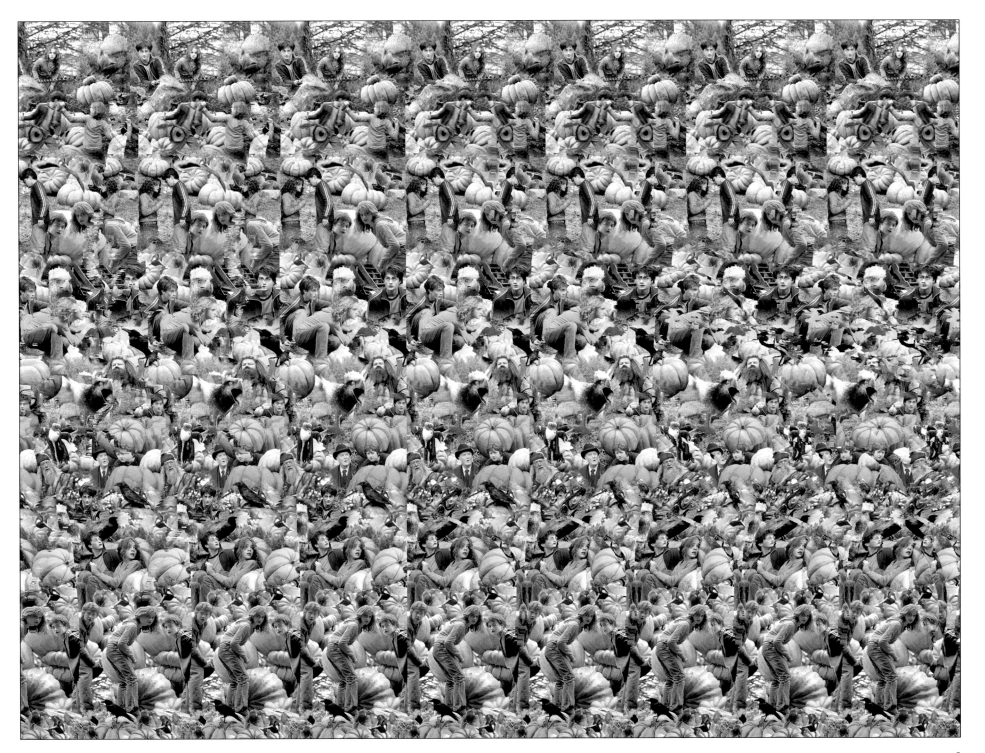

5

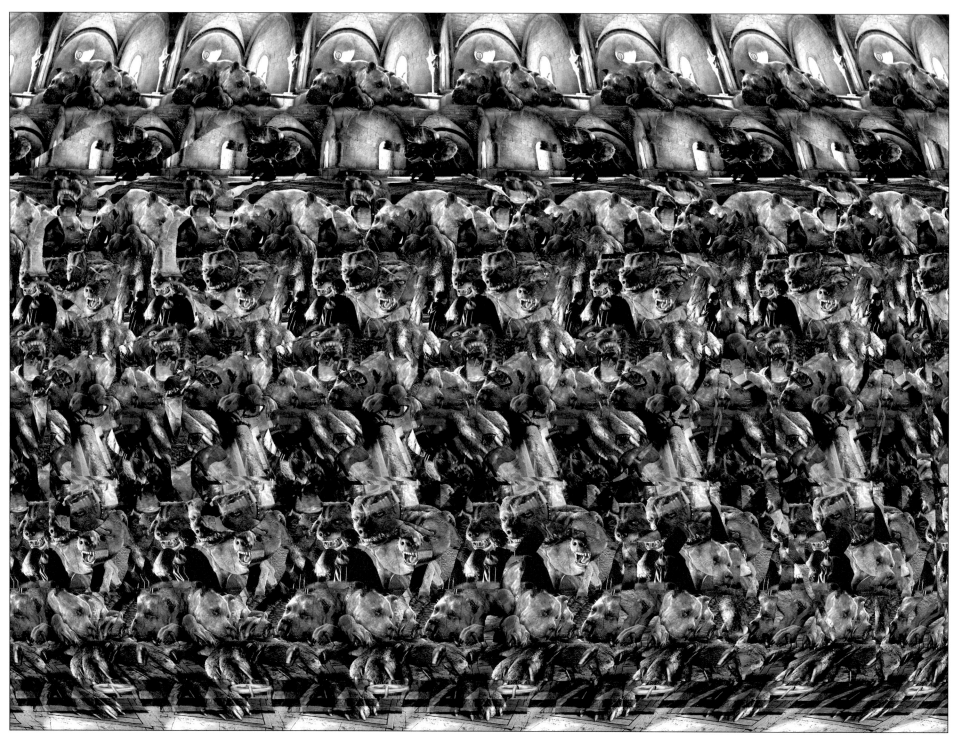

6

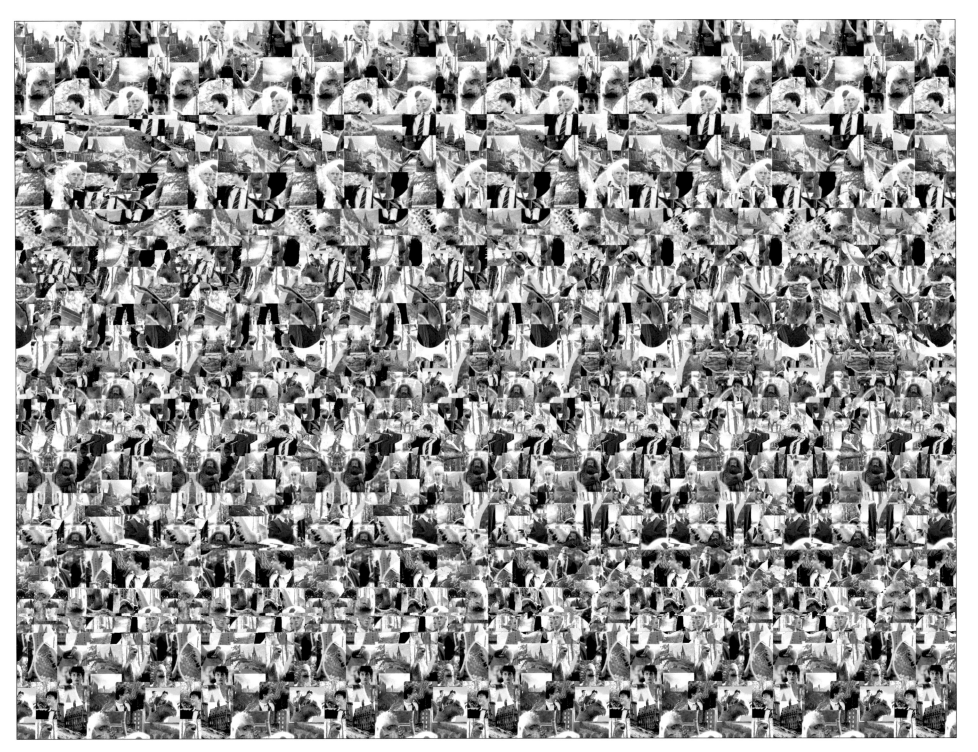

9

10

13

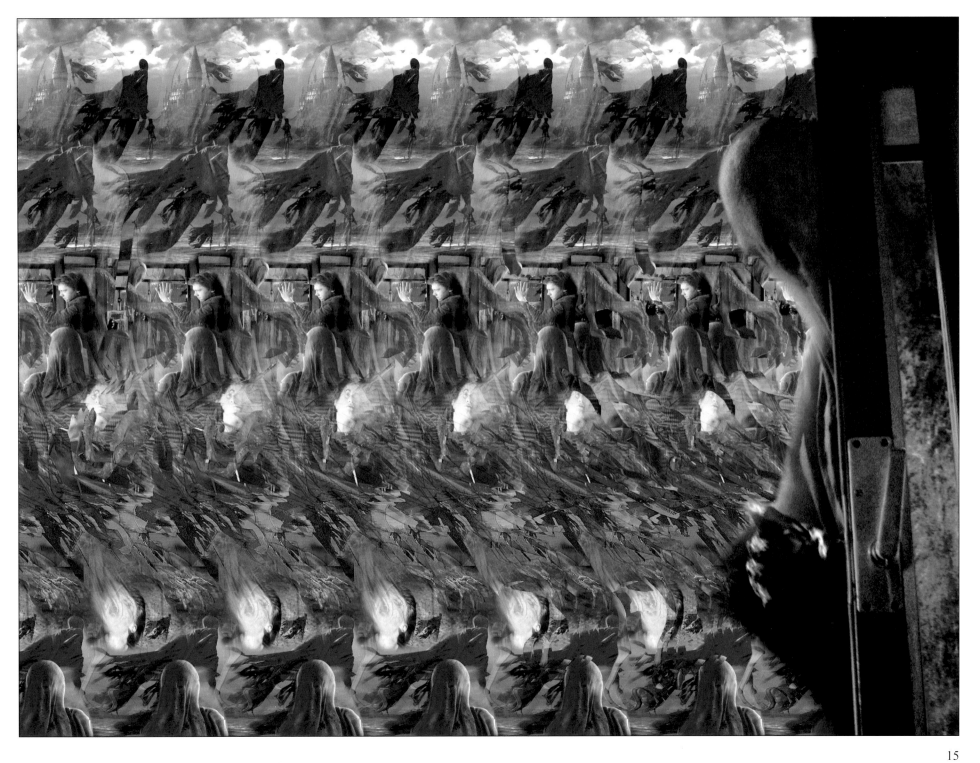

15

16

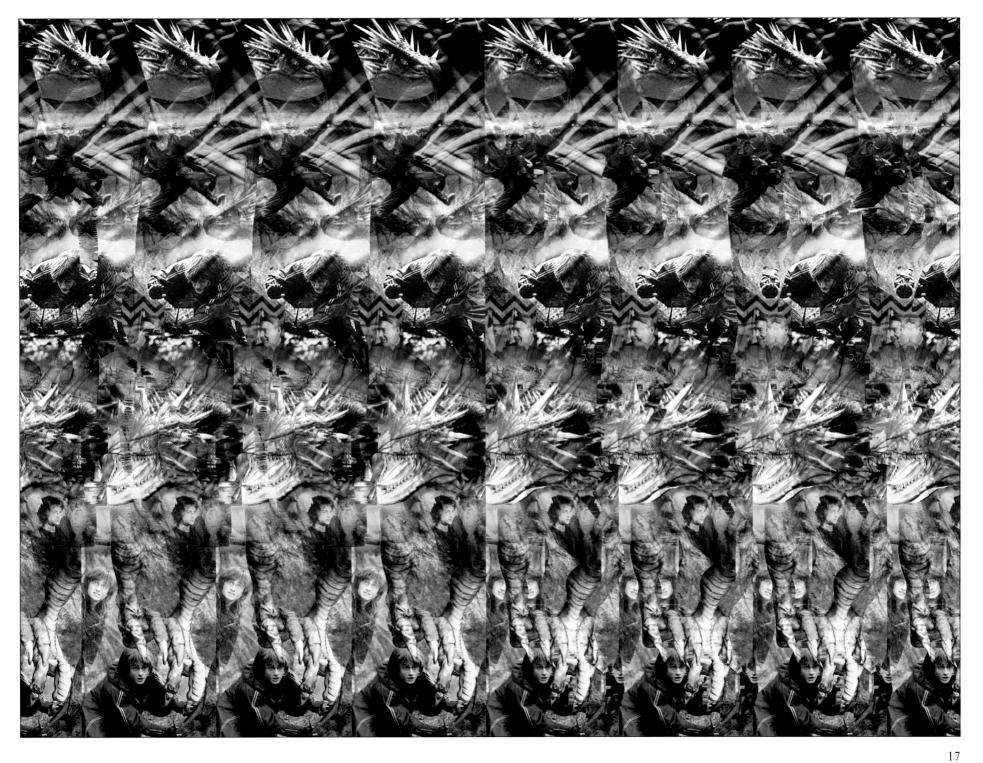

17

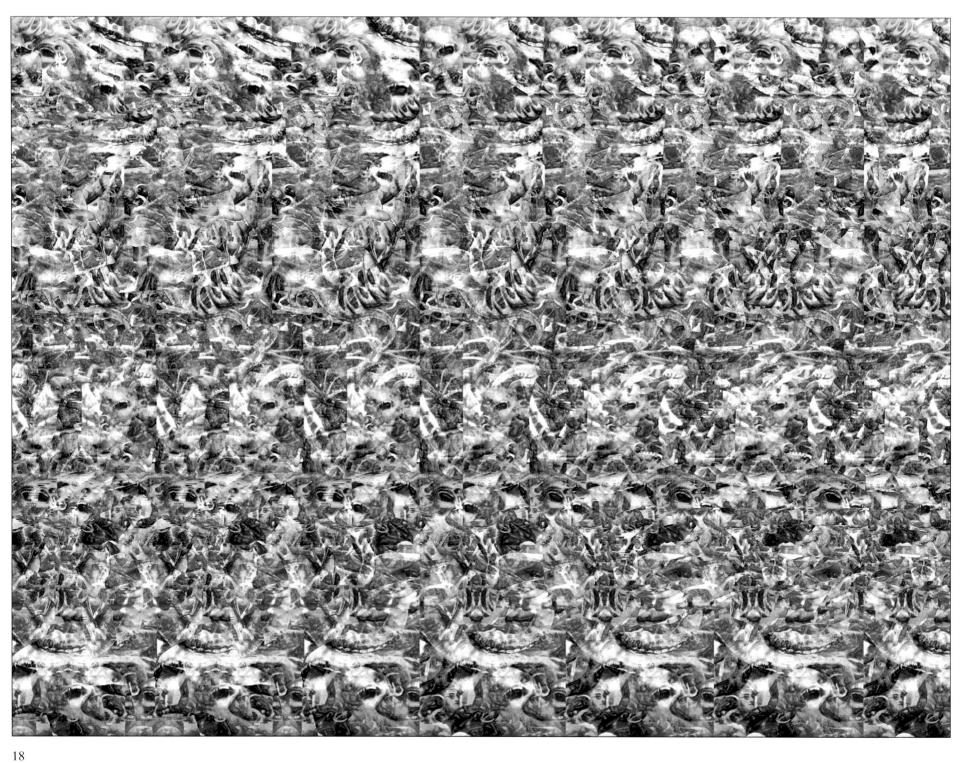

18

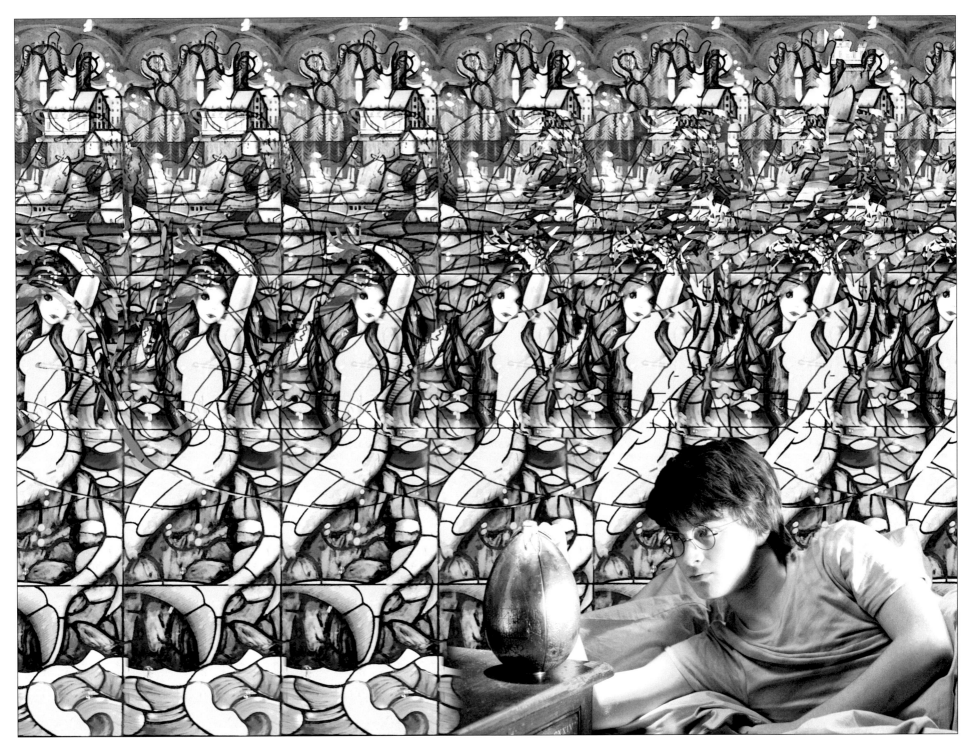

20

22

23

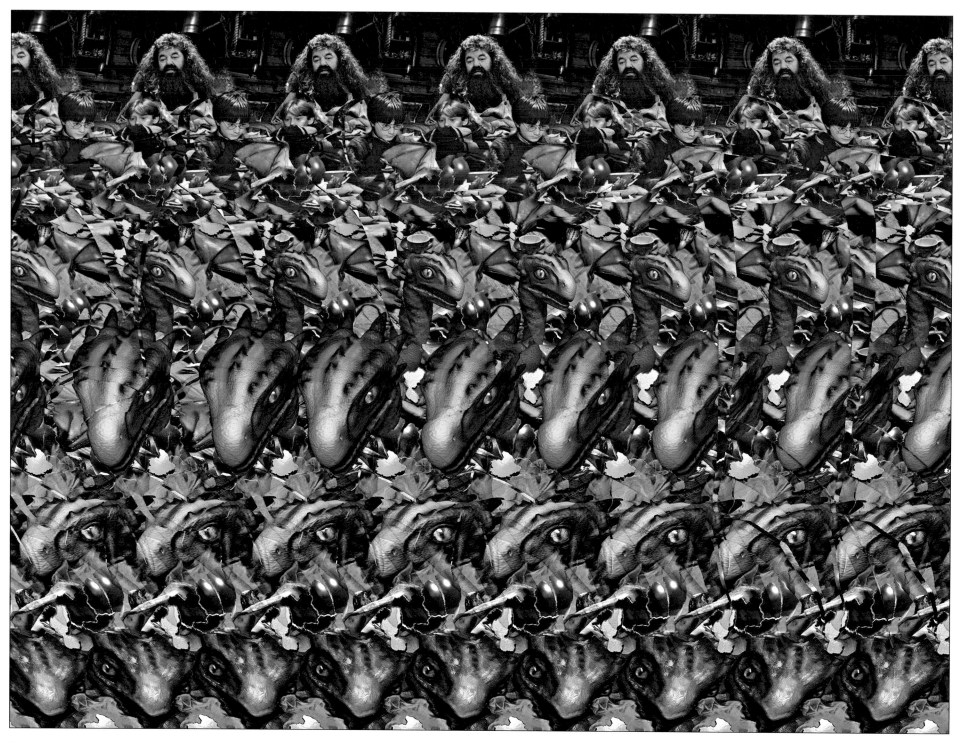

Book Cover
Hedwig

Page 4
3D Viewing Instructions

Page 5   Buckbeak™ (Rescue)

Page 6   Fluffy

Page 7   Goblin

Page 8   Cornish Pixie

Page 9   Buckbeak™ (Flying)

Page 10   Troll

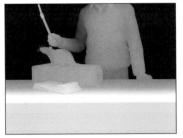

Page 11   Scabbers™

Page 12   Dobby™

Page 13   Fang

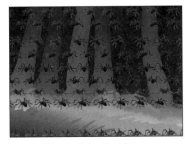

Page 14   Spiders

Page 15   Dementor™

Page 16   Dobby™ (Freedom)

Page 17   Hungarian
Horntail Dragon

Page 18   Grindylows

Page 19   Mermaid

Page 20   Thestral

Page 21   Werewolf

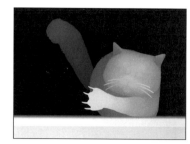

Page 22   Crookshanks™

Page 23   Mandrake

Page 24   Norbert

Page 25   Hedwig™

Page 26   Nagini

Page 27   Centaur

Page 28   Basilisk

Page 29   Fawkes™

Page 30   Stag Patronus